BAREFOOT BOOKS

The barefoot child symbolises the human being whose natural integrity and

capacity for action are unimpaired. In this spirit, Barefoot Books publishes

new and traditional myths, legends and fairy tales whose themes demonstrate

the pitfalls and dangers that surround our passage through life; the qualities

that are needed to face and overcome these dangers; and the equal importance

of action and reflection in doing so. Our intention is to present stories from a

wide range of cultures in such a way as to delight and inspire readers of all

ages while honouring the tradition from which the story has been inherited.

Barefoot Books Ltd
PO Box 95
Kingswood
Bristol BS15 5BH

Graphic design by Design/Section

Printed in Great Britain by Butler & Tanner Ltd, Frome

ISBN 1 898000 90 5

Dedicated to:

Alex Horne

My parents, Kay and Eileen Tse

My nephews and nieces, Jason and Louisa Leung

and Catherine and Daniel Tse,

Polka Theatre for Children, London

Janet and Veronica Needa

Karty Sherbourne

Kim Teoh

My publisher, Tessa Strickland

My copy-editor, Kate Parker

THE MAGIC PAINTBRUSH

Adapted from the
Chinese Fable by

DAVID K. S. TSE

BAREFOOT BOOKS

FOREWORD

T his book was written because Roman Stefanski, Associate Director at the Polka Theatre, London, enjoyed the original Chinese fable, and Vicky Ireland, Artistic Director at Polka, had faith to commission me to adapt a stage version for Polka. My publisher, Tessa Strickland, heard about the play and had the courage to commission this, my first children's book.

I researched the story in London and Hong Kong, in English and Chinese. The original author is unknown because the fable was told by oral storytellers, who would travel from village to village in China and recite their magical tales to entertain, comfort and inspire their audiences. It is interesting to note that the standard version of the story from mainland China now casts the chief villain as a corrupt official, whereas the version I found in Hong Kong casts him as the Emperor, which I much preferred.

I loved magic and fantasy when I read books as a child, and

the idea of the Magic Paintbrush conjured up wonderful images. The fact that it could only help poor people made me think of the story's hero, Ma Leung, as a sort of Chinese 'Robin Hood'. The magic provided a great escape into a fantasy world, but I differ from the original because, in the end, I wanted Ma Leung to have learnt something from his experiences and to step back into reality, without the Magic Paintbrush.

I also added the spirits of his parents and his two friends, Siu Yeen and Fay Ma, to keep Ma Leung company. His hermit-like existence depicted in the original story was based on Taoist or Buddhist teachings – I have kept these elements in my version by having Ma Leung choose his own 'way' or path to find his destiny (a feature of Taoism), and by making Siu Yeen a Buddhist.

Ma Leung is the archetypal Chinese child-hero: long-suffering, yet resourceful and kind, with a 'good heart'. I made him a bit more mischievous, so that he is as much of a child as a hero. I also made him homeless to remind readers of our own housing shortages.

In the original story, the ghost Bac Wu only appears when he gives the Magic Paintbrush to Ma Leung. I wanted him to have more importance, particularly because ancestor worship is a common Chinese custom. I also connected Bac Wu with the tyrannical Emperor Wong Dai by making them brothers.

The original story's themes of greed and justice fitted well with my debate about the morality of revenge – a common Chinese theme; and the final overthrow of a ruthless Chinese autocrat will have modern resonances for anyone who followed the events of Tiananmen Square on 4 June 1989.

I added to the story the ancient practice of binding girls' feet, so as to highlight the cruelty of the Emperor. In reality, only wealthy families bound their daughters' feet, in order to flaunt their standing in society by showing that their daughters did not have to engage in domestic labour.

In ancient China, women were not allowed to take a job, following the teachings of Confucius that a woman's place was in the home. However, I have introduced two female characters who subvert this historical fact: one is Ma Leung's beloved former art teacher, and the other is the wicked landlady Ah Ying, who is a cross between the Peking Opera's 'Woman Warrior' and Cruella de Vil. I did not want both the villains in the story to be men.

I have included the occasional Chinese word or phrase, to honour the original language of the story. Such phrases are written phonetically in English, following a system devised by myself (and reflecting the fact that I speak Cantonese) rather than an established method such as the Pinyin System. I have added translations of the Chinese words in notes whenever they occur. Do not be surprised that some Chinese names have a meaning: Ma Leung means 'Good Horse', for instance.

T'ai chi (a meditative martial art) and fung shui (literally 'wind and water', a Taoist way of predicting the future) are respected Chinese practices, but I have ironically given them to Seen San, the buffoon of an art teacher. The ninja are traditional Japanese spies, but their all-black clothing and martial skill seemed to provide a suitable description for Siu Yeen when she tries to rescue Ma Leung from the Palace.

Of course, I wanted the story to be fun, and I have given the Magic Paintbrush a cheeky personality, whereas the original character had no 'life'.

I hope that I have told this new version of the story in the same spirit as that of the old Chinese storytellers, and that you will enjoy reading it as much I have enjoyed writing it.

David K. S. Tse
London, 1994

CHAPTER 1

Long ago in the Middle Kingdom of China, when dragons surfed on waves and phoenixes danced on clouds, there lived a young orphan boy named Ma Leung.[1] His elderly parents had died during a particularly harsh winter, and, with no relatives to help pay the rent, Ma Leung's house had been confiscated by the local landlady in Canton.

    1 Good Horse

In order to survive, Ma Leung worked very hard selling firewood in the market, but he never earned much, and sometimes, if he had been unlucky, Ma Leung would go to bed with his tummy rumbling and his heart feeling empty. He slept in the open air under the stars, with only a grey blanket to keep him warm and a giant banyan tree to shelter him from the rain.

Sometimes the spirits of Ma Leung's parents would visit him, and they would cry because they were unable to help their son. They would stroke his hair without actually touching him and pray to Kuan Yin, the Goddess of Mercy, for an end to the boy's suffering. Reluctantly, they would return to the spirit world at the first rays of dawn.

Despite his circumstances, Ma Leung was strong and cheerful. After work, he would either play with his two friends, Siu Yeen[2] and Fay Ma,[3] or indulge in his favourite passion – art. More than anything in the world, Ma Leung wanted to be a great painter but, since he could not afford to buy a paintbrush, he had to content himself with drawing.

2 Little Swallow   **3 Flying Horse**

All of Ma Leung's pictures were inspired by nature. He used charred pieces of twig to draw on the banyan tree and, when that was covered, he drew in the dirt or on the mud of the riverbank. He used wet reeds to draw on flat stones, and even created some simple watercolours by crushing wild berries, or by squeezing the juice out of vegetables.

Ma Leung practised drawing every day, so that his pictures became very life-like. Yet, all the time, Ma Leung yearned for a real paintbrush.

CHAPTER 2

The wind had changed. Thunder rumbled and quaked in the heavens, and a dark cloud hung over the Middle Kingdom. The Great Phoenix screeched and swooped to pluck out the eyes of the Golden Dragon, which leapt out of the sea to do battle with her. They fought in the heavens in a flurry of feathers, and in the ocean depths amidst a ball of flame.

Then the mighty Yellow River burst her banks, and Famine and Pestilence stalked the land. Rumours spread of increased sightings of ghosts and disturbed ancestors, so the people lit incense and burnt paper offerings to appease the gods, praying to Kuan Yin and to Lord Buddha to save them.

The kind old Emperor had died, and his brother, the new Emperor, was ruthless. He taxed poor peasants heavily, but allowed wealthy landlords and court officials to make big profits. Life grew harder for Ma Leung as the villagers had less money to buy his firewood.

One midnight, in the midst of these troubles, the ghost of an
I White Beard old man appeared. Bac Wu' was dressed in white, with a long
flowing beard and no feet. He continually repeated the same
refrain, over and over:

> 'I am searching
> I am searching
> For a child of heaven
> With a pure heart
> And a clear conscience.
>
> A child who has nothing
> But can give everything
> I am searching
> I am searching
> For this child of heaven.
>
> A gift I bring
> From the Goddess of Mercy
> A gift most rare
> A thing of beauty
> For this child of heaven.
>
> When gift and child are united at last
> Then shall earth shake, and tyrants all pass
> Into emptiness.'

Bac Wu flew past the banyan tree and mistook the grey mass
under it for a rock. In fact, it was Ma Leung, hidden under his
blanket, fast asleep. Bac Wu continued his weary search.

CHAPTER 3

'Wake up, or you'll be late for work.' Siu Yeen, Ma Leung's best friend, was calling to him.

The boy woke up with difficulty. 'Morning,' he yawned, grinning at the same time.

Siu Yeen often woke Ma Leung up with a warn coconut bun or Chinese egg custard tart for his breakfast. Her parents were peasant farmers who suffered under the high taxes imposed by the new Emperor, so Siu Yeen risked being scolded by them whenever she secretly helped her friend.

'How are you today?' asked Siu Yeen.

'Cold,' replied Ma Leung. 'It was freezing last night!'

'Yes. Winter seems to be early this year, and the mornings are so gloomy. I've brought you a spare blanket.' She handed it to him.

'Thanks.' He grinned again. 'You're a real Buddhist.'

'Don't tease me!' She gave him a painful Chinese burn to prove that she was not a goody-goody.

'Ouch! Where did you learn to do that?'

'From a Buddhist nun!'

Ma Leung playfully jumped on her, and they rolled about, mock-fighting. Suddenly a piercing cry, high in the sky, stopped their cavorting, and they looked up to see a golden eagle hovering, hunting, ready to pounce on some unsuspecting prey.

'Look!' cried Ma Leung. 'She thinks my chicken drawing is real!' Quick as a flash, he rushed over to a drawing he had made in the dirt the day before, and wiped it away. The eagle screeched her disappointment, beat her wings and soared away in search of a more substantial victim.

'Baa, baa, baaaaaaa!' Some sheep had stumbled across Ma Leung's wolf drawing and, in their panic to escape, they crashed into the two children.

'It's only a picture, you silly sheep!' laughed Siu Yeen , as she wiped away Ma Leung's charcoal drawing. She looked at her friend with pride.

'Your drawings are so good that even the animals are fooled! You'd be better with a paintbrush, because then you could add lovely colours and make things look even more realistic.'

'Yes, that's how I feel,' replied Ma Leung, 'but I don't have a paintbrush, so I'll never become a great painter!'

'Don't worry. If it's meant to be, then it will happen. Trust me.' With that, Siu Yeen set off to school, leaving Ma Leung to ponder over her words. A cry of 'Gai-see! Market-time!' roused

him from his thoughts, and he hurried off to sell his firewood.

CHAPTER 4

As Ma Leung walked to the market, it started to drizzle. He took a different path and passed his old school, which he had attended when his parents were alive and could pay the fees. This was where he had met Siu Yeen. This was also where he had first tried his hand at painting and discovered how much fun it was. And it was somewhere he could shelter from the rain.

Ma Leung wondered if his old art teacher still taught there. She had encouraged Ma Leung to follow in the old Emperor's footsteps, since his Majesty was reputed to be the greatest painter in China; though no commoner had ever seen the Emperor's paintings, because the Imperial Palace was the 'Forbidden City', and out of bounds.

Ma Leung remembered his old teacher's kind heart, and he wanted to thank her. Ma Leung also wanted to ask whether he could perhaps borrow a paintbrush, if only for a short time, so that he could paint. He felt sure that the teacher would understand. None the less, Ma Leung had to screw up his courage and put the state of his clothes to the back of his mind, before going in. To his disappointment, he found a different teacher at the head of the class.

'Now if you pay close attention to what I'm doing, you may learn something. First of all, you adopt a stance like this,' said the new teacher, Seen San,[1] twisting his body into a t'ai chi[2] position. 'Then you centre yourself by humming deeply...Hmmm...Balance the paintbrush like a fine sword and let the natural forces of wind and water guide your creative juices...Hmmm...'

Seen San closed his eyes and became very still. Ma Leung wondered if he was ill. Suddenly Seen San launched his body into a frenzy of activity, and in an instant it was all over. The class crowded round to look at his canvas, and little gasps of delight and wonderment came from their young lips. Ma Leung joined them quietly, then burst into laughter when he saw Seen San's work.

'And who are you?' asked Seen San pointedly.

'Excuse me...ha ha...lay-ho[3]...hee hee...' Ma Leung gestured formally with his hands, trying desperately to stop laughing. 'My name is Ma Leung, and...tee hee...I used to study here under a different teacher and—'

1 Teacher
2 Chinese martial art

3 Chinese greeting

'What is so funny?' Seen San demanded.

'Em…well, why have you made funny squiggles on your paper?' Now it was Ma Leung's turn to be laughed at. The class and Seen San roared at his ignorance, and Ma Leung turned bright red with embarrassment.

'My dear boy, the "funny squiggles" are calligraphy. I have painted my name as beautifully as possible, and the result is most aesthetically pleasing, would you not say?'

'No,' replied Ma Leung bluntly. 'Where's the beauty in painting your name? A poem or proverb, now that I can understand, but your name? Are you famous or something?'

'You peasants will never understand. Get out!'

'But I want to borrow a paintbrush!' pleaded Ma Leung hopelessly.

'Out, I say! How dare you come in here and beg, you little tramp! Out!' Seen San's eyes were bulging like a mad dog's, and Ma Leung wondered if indeed the man was sick.

'But—'

Ma Leung's words were cut off by a huge glob of mucous which the hysterical Seen San spat into his face. Silent shock, disgust and rage all welled up in Ma Leung. Very calmly, he wiped his face clean and said: 'You are an immature idiot, not fit to teach children.'

Then Ma Leung quickly spat back in Seen San's face, kicked

him in the shin and ran off. The class were left speechless: all that Seen San had taught them about Confucian obedience was shattered in one moment by a young stranger.

As Ma Leung rounded the brow of the hill towards market, he thought he heard cheers coming from the school and the sound of chairs being thrown through windows.

CHAPTER 5

At the market, Ma Leung was preoccupied by thoughts about the new art teacher. 'I'll show him! I'll be a famous painter one day, and then he'll be sorry, the stingy so-and-so!' He was furious about the way Seen San had behaved, and the steady rain which now fell on him did not help his mood.

Ma Leung was also having no luck selling his firewood. The villagers were finding it hard to keep up with their rents, and some had been made homeless by the local landlady. Others complained bitterly about the high taxes, yet they all felt unable to challenge the might of the new Emperor. Most people remembered the old Emperor with affection and longing, and his reign as a time of peace and prosperity.

'Firewood! Buy your firewood here! The best value in Canton!' cried Ma Leung.

'How much?' demanded a frail old woman.

'Five yuan¹ will buy you a whole bundle of firewood.'   **1 Chinese money**

'Too much!' she replied curtly. 'I can't afford it.'

'Well, how about four yuan?' Ma Leung suggested.

'Less, less!' she retorted, 'or I'll freeze to death!'

'What can you afford, then? Don't forget, mine is the best wood in Canton. I gathered it from the highest mountains...'

'Yes, yes,' said the old woman dismissively, 'I'm sure you did, but now it's wet and probably the worst. Anyway, I can only afford to pay you two yuan. The landlady has taken the rest of my money for this week.'

Ma Leung thought long and hard. Two yuan was not enough to buy a decent dinner, and he loathed the thought of another night with his belly rumbling. But the old woman did look very frail, which reminded him of his mother when she was near death, and he felt sorry for her. Besides, she was the only customer he had had all day, and for that he felt grateful to her.

'All right. Here!' Ma Leung handed her a bundle of firewood for her money. 'Keep warm!'

'Thank you, young man,' said the old woman. 'You have a good heart.' She hobbled away.

Ma Leung looked around the market for some food he could afford to buy, but nearly everything was too expensive, and nobody was feeling charitable. In the end, he settled for a stick of sugar-cane, which he sucked very slowly to make it last, as he walked home.

'Pppppp!' A horse blew his lips behind Ma Leung, causing the boy's wet hair to ruffle and making him jump. Ma Leung spun around.

'Fay Ma! I haven't seen you for a long time.' The boy threw his arms around the stallion's neck and hugged him hard.

'Are you hungry? Yes? Here, you can have the rest of this.' Ma Leung gave his sugar-cane to the delighted horse. The boy patted and stroked his friend, and tried to ignore his protesting, rumbling tummy.

Unknown to Ma Leung, he was being watched. Bac Wu, the ghost, had observed Ma Leung's actions and was growing excited. But before he had a chance to introduce himself, Ma Leung jumped on Fay Ma's back and shouted:

'Fly, fly, be swift and bold,
Race through the air
On wings of gold!'

The stallion galloped away with Ma Leung laughing on his back. Bac Wu gave chase, but to no avail. Not even a ghost could catch Fay Ma, the fastest wild horse in China.

CHAPTER 6

An exhausted, gasping Bac Wu finally came across the banyan tree at midnight. He had followed Fay Ma's hoof marks all the way, and, in the light of a full moon, Bac Wu saw the sleeping boy and his trusty friend nearby. The rain had died down and all was still. Hugely relieved, Bac Wu looked up and smiled at Kuan Yin, the Goddess of Mercy, who congratulated him on finding the child by sending down a beam of rainbow light. Bac Wu repeated his refrain quietly – 'I am searching, I am searching…' – to wake up Ma Leung very gently. The boy stirred: 'What's happening? Where am I? Fay Ma!'

He had seen Bac Wu floating just above the ground. Fay Ma woke with a start and whinnied with horror at the ghost. Bac Wu hovered in the air, safely out of reach.

'Be calm, be still; I bring no ill
But joy on earth for all to feel
A vessel I am for the Goddess of Mercy
Bearing a gift with powers aplenty.

You are the child
I've searched long and hard for
To deliver my people
From a yoke
Unbearable.

What does the child of heaven desire?
The gift – you must choose it
The act – you must do it.

Revenge is wrong and inexcusable
But tyranny is worse and unforgivable.

Choose your gift, fulfil your destiny
The people of China ache for liberty
When gift and child are united at last
Then shall earth shake, and tyrants all pass
Into emptiness.'

Ma Leung rubbed his eyes and pinched himself to check that he
was awake. His ears were filled with a magical tinkling sound, as
if the stars had become wind chimes, or each individual water-

drop from the stream was tumbling in slow motion over the smooth pebbles.

'Who are you?' Ma Leung asked.

'A lover of painting
A failed Emperor
A murdered brother
An avenging ghost.

A healer of pain
A fighter for justice
A speaker of truth
A catalyst –
Bac Wu is my name.'

'Well, Bac Wu,' replied Ma Leung shakily, 'what I really want is a paintbrush.'

Without further ado, Bac Wu cupped his hands to form a lotus flower, and all the rainbow light came together into his palms. It took shape and turned into a burst of white light which dazzled Ma Leung and Fay Ma. When the light had faded, Bac Wu was left holding an impressive paintbrush. It sparkled like diamonds. Ceremonially, he handed it to Ma Leung with the following advice:

'Follow a path of earth and truth

True gold is precious and always shared

Power is a dangerous tool

Use this gift with wisdom and care.

Bo sow[1] for my spirit

Set the people free

Let the Magic Paintbrush

Paint your destiny.'

1 Take revenge

'Oh, thank you, Bac Wu! Dor-tse,[2] sher-sher!'[3] exclaimed Ma Leung. He rushed forward to hug Bac Wu but, when he opened his eyes, Ma Leung found he was hugging himself in the dark. A wind chilled him to the bone.

'It was just a dream, Fay Ma. Just another silly dream.'

The stallion pawed at the ground impatiently. Curious, Ma Leung rushed over and then screamed with delight. It was real! There lay his Magic Paintbrush! The boy felt dizzy with joy, and he and Fay Ma danced and jumped in wild circles. Then he calmed himself and reverently approached the Magic Paintbrush. Ma Leung picked it up, lifting it with difficulty – for such a small thing, it was surprisingly heavy. He raised it slowly and held it high above his head like a conquering sword, then shouted into the night sky ablaze with stars:

4 Paintbrush

'My Wac Buc![4] My Magic Paintbrush!'

2 'Thank you' in Cantonese (in response to a gift)

3 'Thank you' in Mandarin – the official Chinese language (which Ma Leung is using in order to emphasise his gratitude)

CHAPTER 7

Under the gaze of the moon and stars, Ma Leung set off on Fay Ma to tell Siu Yeen his good news, his heart bursting with excitement.

Outside Siu Yeen's farmhouse, Ma Leung dismounted, then paused to think. Her parents would be annoyed if he woke them up so early. Ma Leung decided to paint until the cock crowed.

A low whistle greeted his decision, and Ma Leung looked around suspiciously. Fay Ma had wandered over to a bale of hay and was happily munching. Who else would be up at this hour?

The boy clutched the Magic Paintbrush closely, fearing bandits. The whistle came again, this time more muffled. Ma Leung suddenly realised where the sound was coming from, and he dropped the Magic Paintbrush like a hot potato. Paintbrush squealed with pain. Ma Leung stepped back, wondering if he had killed it. He glanced guiltily at Fay Ma, who had stopped in mid-munch to see what the commotion was.

Slowly, Ma Leung approached the Magic Paintbrush and gingerly picked it up. As he carefully brushed the dust off it, Paintbrush started cooing like a dove. Ma Leung smiled.

'I never knew you could talk,' said the boy.

'There are a lot of things you don't know!' whistled Paintbrush perkily, flying out of Ma Leung's hand and giving him a playful tap on the forehead.

'Why, you…'Ma Leung tried to grab Paintbrush, but it flew nimbly out of his grasp. The boy over-reached, lost his balance and fell over. Fay Ma neighed with laughter, and Paintbrush giggled teasingly. Ma Leung sat up, covered in dirt and straw, saw the others laughing and joined in good-naturedly. Paintbrush flew down and gently brushed the dust out of Ma Leung's face. The boy smiled again.

'Let's do some painting,' he suggested.

Paintbrush whistled brightly and danced a circle. Rainbow light filled the space, and scrolls of delicate rice-paper flew down from the heavens and hovered in the air. Ma Leung touched one, and its texture seemed to say: 'Paint on me.' Ma Leung seized the Magic Paintbrush as if he had been born with it, and started to paint.

A peacock gradually appeared, shimmering with colour and life. Then, when Ma Leung applied the last stroke to his painting, an extraordinary thing happened. The peacock was submerged in a shroud of white light, and Ma Leung's ears were filled with heavenly music, which ended with the crash of a loud gong. Following this, there came a ripping sound of tearing paper, and, to Ma Leung's and Fay Ma's astonishment, a real peacock emerged from the paper and flew up into the night sky, dropping one of its feathers as a token of thanks.

After Ma Leung had caught his breath, he painted a golden carp. Once again, at the last stroke, the same thing happened. The lucky goldfish wriggled out of the paper and flip-flopped on the ground, gasping for water. Ma Leung quickly picked it up and carried it safely to the stream, where it dived deeply and then resurfaced, blowing bubbles of gratitude to the boy.

Ma Leung laughed and clapped for joy. Fay Ma shared in his friend's happiness by neighing and dancing with Paintbrush, and, finally, when they were all spent, they lay down together and fell asleep. Ma Leung slept better than he had since his parents died, and his dreams were full of dancing paintbrushes with ribbons of trailing paint, making his parents clap and cry with laughter and joy.

CHAPTER 8

'Wake up, Ma Leung, or you'll be late for work.' It was Siu Yeen. Ma Leung was supposed to work even on Saturdays. 'Why are you sleeping here?'

'Hello,' grinned the boy, with such an air of smugness that Siu Yeen knew something was afoot. She gave him a Chinese burn to bring him back down to earth.

'Ouch!' But this time, Ma Leung did not mock-fight with her.

'What's wrong?' Siu Yeen was concerned.

'Nothing. Look, I have something wonderful to show you.' Ma Leung produced the Magic Paintbrush and Siu Yeen gasped.

'Where did you get that from?' she asked. 'I hope you haven't stolen it.' She knew how badly Ma Leung needed to paint.

'Of course not, silly. I was given it last night in a dream…No – I mean, this ghost called Bac Wu gave it to me as a gift from the Goddess of Mercy. He called me a "child of heaven" and said that I was to destroy tyrants with it. He wants me to bo sow¹ for   ¹ Take reveng him, and I think he was the old Emperor of China!'

'How much sleep did you have last night?' asked Siu Yeen.

'Why?'

'Because maybe you need to lie down somewhere and—'

'I'm fine!' Ma Leung was indignant. 'Look, you're supposed
to be Buddhist and believe these things. This has never
happened to me before, and I want you to understand. Don't
make fun of me!'

'Sorry,' apologised Siu Yeen. Then, more brightly: 'Hey,
remember how I said, "If it's meant to be, then it will happen"?
Well, now that it has, surely it means that you'll end up a
famous painter!'

'Yes, but there's more to it than that,' added Ma Leung. 'You
see, this is no ordinary paintbrush. It possesses powerful magic
which can be very dangerous – Bac Wu warned me about that.'

'What sort of magic?' Siu Yeen's eyes were gleaming.

'When I paint things, they come alive,' explained Ma Leung.
Try as hard as she might, Siu Yeen could not help laughing.
Then she wondered if he was playing another of his jokes on her.

'All right, I'll show you if you don't believe me.'

Quickly, Ma Leung painted an enormous spider, horribly
hairy with two big fangs. When the creature came to life, Siu
Yeen screamed blue murder and clambered on to Fay Ma for
protection.

'I believe you, I believe you!' she shouted. 'Now make it go away!'

Ma Leung's laughter died as he realised that he did not know how to banish the spider. The hairy thing studied Ma Leung with its large bug eyes, then suddenly charged at him, fangs gnashing. Now it was Ma Leung's turn to scream and beat a hasty retreat.

'A hole! Paint a bottomless pit, quick!' screamed Siu Yeen.

Ma Leung followed his friend's advice, just as the spider was catching up with his trailing foot. Even its eight legs could not stop the spider from plunging into the bottomless pit. Ma Leung immediately sealed up the hole, and everyone breathed a sigh of relief.

'I'm sorry—'

'No, I'm sorry for not trusting you in the first place,' said Siu Yeen. 'Your paintbrush is incredible.'

'I suppose that's what Bac Wu meant about using the Magic Paintbrush wisely and carefully.'

'What else did he say?' asked Siu Yeen.

'That I must help him to bo sow.'

'Take revenge on what?'

'I'm not sure,' shrugged Ma Leung. 'Tyrants?'

The sky suddenly darkened and thunder rumbled menacingly in the distance. The two children looked up, perturbed.

'Well, you can't go around taking revenge on just anybody,'

Siu Yeen observed. 'Forgive and forget, that's what Lord Buddha taught.'

'All right, smarty-pants. What do you suggest we do instead, then?'

'Well, how about painting something for yourself first?'

'Good idea! Paintbrush!' The Magic Paintbrush whistled to attention.

'It talks too!' exclaimed Siu Yeen.

'Of course, silly. It's magic!'

Ma Leung set to work, this time without any paper, as he wanted to master the art of using the Magic Paintbrush by itself. He made large brush strokes, fluid and strong, using his whole body as though he were dancing, and, at the last stroke, the magic still happened. Rainbow light filled the space, heavenly music rang out and a loud gong set off blazing white light, which, when it cooled, revealed a modest but elegant house.

'Now we're neighbours!' beamed Ma Leung.

'Fantastic!' Siu Yeen's mouth was still open with amazement.

'Time for some new clothes,' laughed Ma Leung. In an instant, he and Siu Yeen were standing in bright new clothes of red and green. She hugged him with delight.

'Come on,' he said. 'Let's see what the village people need.' The two friends hopped on to Fay Ma and galloped into town.

CHAPTER 9

There was a break in the clouds as the three friends arrived in the market square. The children gathered a large crowd together and explained the Magic Paintbrush's powers. Despite their poverty, most of the villagers were proud and they made rude remarks. Only one farmer, too poor to care any more about what people thought, stepped forward.

'I can't buy seeds to grow food because all my money is spent on rent and the Emperor's tax. Please, if you can do it, paint me some rice plants, so I can grow them in my paddy field.'

Ma Leung granted the farmer his wish, bringing tears of relief to the tired man's eyes. The villagers were astounded. Forgetting their pride, they crowded forward to receive help from Ma Leung. The boy helped one old couple with some new chairs, and another with a hoe; others needed an ox to plough their field; the hungry were fed and the sick supplied with practical items such as crutches or bandages.

News of this god-like boy spread rapidly, and soon throngs of desperate people were pushing and shoving to reach him, despite Fay Ma and Siu Yeen's attempts to keep them in order. Ma Leung was perilously hemmed in, and in danger of being crushed. Siu Yeen shouted to him to be careful, but her cries were drowned out by the clamour of the crowd and the roar of approaching thunder.

She sent Fay Ma home to fetch her parents, just as the heavens opened and buckets of rain came chucking down. But this did not dampen the crowd's fervour – instead, they became even more heated. Siu Yeen decided that she could not wait for her parents' help. Using her Wing Chun[1] training, she fought her way into the mob to rescue her friend.

Ma Leung was busy painting whatever was demanded, as quickly as he could, to save himself from being completely crushed.

Just as everything seemed to be lost, the crowd miraculously parted, and a blaze of lightning revealed the silhouette of an elegant, agile-looking woman with a staff of bamboo. As the stranger hammered her staff into the ground with an angry cry, the thunder crashed and the earth shook. The villagers were petrified, and many of them scampered away, shouting: 'Ah Ying, Ah Ying!'[2] Those too stubborn to leave were beaten with her stick, until all the scavengers had left. Ma Leung and Siu Yeen huddled

1 A style of martial art developed by a Chinese nun

2 Golden Eagle

together, shaking with fright and cold.

'Th...th...thank you,' stammered Ma Leung.

'Y...yes, mm...mm-goy,'[3] chattered Siu Yeen. Then, after

3 'Thank you' in Cantonese

swallowing hard to calm herself, she asked: 'Who are you?'

'My name is Ah Ying, or "Golden Eagle", if you prefer, or even, as some people call me, "the wicked witch of a landlady"!'

Ma Leung and Siu Yeen exchanged looks. Both of them found it hard to believe that their rescuer was the bad woman they had heard so many stories about.

'My name means "Good Horse",' offered Ma Leung.

'And mine's "Little Swallow",' added Siu Yeen.

'Well, I'm very pleased to meet you both – in one piece!' Ah Ying chuckled at her tasteless joke. 'I can see you've been very shaken by your little adventure.'

'I never realised we'd cause so much trouble,' Ma Leung confessed.

'Well, why don't you come home with me for some tea and cake? That'll warm you up and calm you both down. You'd like that, wouldn't you? Come along now.'

Before the children had a chance to consider or object, Ah Ying swept them along in her strong arms. The rain fell steadily down.

CHAPTER 10

It was still raining when they arrived at Ah Ying's grand house. Two bumbling servants, Sor Ji[1] and Sor Gai,[2] guarded the entrance. Sor Ji had the face of a pig, while Sor Gai seemed to strut about like a chicken. Ma Leung found them very funny, but Siu Yeen was distracted and in no laughing mood.

1 Stupid Pig

2 Silly Chicken

'I'm an official of the Emperor,' Ah Ying explained, as she ordered her servants inside to prepare tea and cakes for her guests. The children exchanged another furtive look, and Siu Yeen's brow furrowed.

Inside, Ah Ying's house smelt of comfort and refinement. Two jade lions guarded a large portrait of the Emperor, the ancestral shrine was carved from marble, and her statue of Buddha made of gold. Tasteful porcelain ornaments stood on a lacquered wooden chest, and the central table and chairs were made of blackwood and huali.[3]

3 Chinese hardwood

The two children sat awkwardly in the massive chairs and felt as if they had wandered into a giant's house by mistake. They watched Sor Ji smacking his lips as he brought out the cakes. Sor Gai nearly tripped over when he brought the jasmine tea. Ah Ying dismissed them irritably. She lit three incense sticks at the shrine, to thank the gods for delivering the children into her hands, and then poured tea.

'Good health and prosperity!' she gushed. The children smiled weakly. Siu Yeen's unease had communicated itself to Ma Leung, who peered at his tea with trepidation, wondering if it was drugged.

'Drink, drink!' urged Ah Ying, sipping her tea with a maternal smile. Since she drank from the same pot, the children felt reassured, and they lightly sipped their tea. The warm, delicate aroma of jasmine soothed the children's fears, and the array of beautiful Chinese cakes brought comfort to their hungry stomachs. Gradually, they began to feel more safe.

'I saw what happened in the market,' said Ah Ying. 'That's some gift you have there!' She laughed, pointing at the Magic Paintbrush. 'You should be careful how you use it.'

'I know! That's what Bac Wu told me,' blurted Ma Leung. Siu Yeen had grown suspicious again and gave Ma Leung a kick under the table.

'Who is Bac Wu?' asked Ah Ying sweetly. Ma Leung

CHAPTER TEN

shrugged. Ah Ying tried another tack. 'You know, I find your Magic Paintbrush absolutely fascinating. Can I have a closer look?'

She reached for Paintbrush, which suddenly flew off the table and painted a cheeky moustache on her face. 'Ah!' she yelled. Paintbrush squealed with delight. Ah Ying summoned her chi[4] and, with a warlike cry, launched herself into battle with the Magic Paintbrush.

4 Internal energy

She went through every kung fu[5] style, from the Tiger to the Crane to the Mantis, but each time Paintbrush would escape and box her ears, tickle her nose or smack her on the bottom. Ah Ying flipped over the table and leapt on to chairs as she tried to catch the Magic Paintbrush, but to no avail.

5 Style of martial art inspired by animal movements

Angry now, she produced her bamboo staff and was about to knock Paintbrush to the ground, when it suddenly grew to five times its original size. The children hid under the table as the two sticks fought it out.

'No!' shouted Ma Leung. But it was too late. Siu Yeen was trying to help the Magic Paintbrush but had underestimated the skill of Ah Ying and her years of disciplined training. The adult spun around and, in one smooth manoeuvre, outwitted Siu Yeen's attack and held the girl in a fierce lock. It was impossible for Siu Yeen to move without causing herself pain, and she felt like a snared rabbit.

'Back off!' Ah Ying ordered Paintbrush, which shrank back to

its usual length and retreated into Ma Leung's hand. The boy
wanted to rescue his friend, but knew that he would be hopeless
against Ah Ying.

'What do you want?' He tried to hide the panic in his voice.

'Quite simple. I want gold. Lots of it. I want to be richer
than the Emperor. Paint me all the gold in China!' Ah Ying's
eyes glistened, and Ma Leung worried for her sanity and Siu
Yeen's safety.

'Fine.' The boy set to work painting, but nothing happened.
He shook the Magic Paintbrush like a blocked fountain pen, but
still it did not work. He squeezed and cajoled it, he cooed at it
and caressed it, but all the magic was gone.

'Don't try any tricks with me, you little shrimp. I can be very
unpleasant.' Ah Ying twisted Siu Yeen's arm tighter, making her
wince with pain.

'Please! Don't hurt her!' Ma Leung was frantic.

'Make it work then!' Ah Ying was losing her patience. Ma
Leung realised he had little time left.

'There's something wrong with it,' he explained as calmly as
possible. 'Maybe it's exhausted after fighting. You need powerful
magic to paint real gold…I think Paintbrush has to rest. The
things I painted for the villagers were all simple – gold takes
more time and energy.'

Ah Ying snatched the Magic Paintbrush out of Ma Leung's

hand and threw Siu Yeen aside. She tried to make Paintbrush work herself, but in vain. The thing seemed limp and helpless. She handed it back in disgust.

'I'll give you till midnight. If it doesn't work then, none of you will see the light of day again – ever.'

With that, Ah Ying picked up the children by the scruff of their necks and marched them into her backyard. The chilly night air had turned the rain to snow, making the children feel more miserable than ever. Ah Ying threw them into her stable and bolted the heavy door with a firm reminder: 'Midnight!'

Ma Leung and Siu Yeen looked at each other, unable to believe that this was happening to them. Then they hugged, and sobbed their hearts out.

CHAPTER 11

'Wah! Ho-doung!'¹ shivered Siu Yeen.

'Yes, I'm freezing too.' Ma Leung rubbed himself to try and keep warm. 'I wonder if the Magic Paintbrush will work now?'

Tentatively, he painted a fire on the stone wall and, to their delight, on the last stroke the fire flickered into life. The children warmed their chilled bodies, and Ma Leung took Paintbrush to task.

'Why didn't you work just now for Ah Ying?'

'Because I can't help greedy people,' whistled Paintbrush.

'But Siu Yeen could have been hurt!' fumed Ma Leung. Paintbrush realised its mistake and cooed apologetically.

'It's all right. Anyone can make a mistake,' said Siu Yeen, stroking Paintbrush and making it purr. Ma Leung was still angry, so the Magic Paintbrush flew over to him and painted a smile on his face, which made Siu Yeen laugh. Then Ma Leung laughed, and Paintbrush blew raspberries to tease him for sulking.

1 It's very cold

'Are you hungry?' asked Ma Leung suddenly.

'Starving!' Siu Yeen nodded.

'Right! Paintbrush, let's create a dinner fit for the heavens!'

The boy and his magical friend danced and jigged, the light dimmed, and gradually, one by one, famous Chinese dishes appeared and joined in the dance.

'Crispy Peking duck!' laughed Ma Leung, as he took a bite at a passing stuffed pancake.

'Monk's vegetables with bean curd!' squealed Siu Yeen, who was a vegetarian.

'Lobster with ginger and spring onion!' drooled Ma Leung.

Chinese broccoli   'Gai-lan[2] with oyster mushrooms!' Siu Yeen was ecstatic.

'All served with fragrant rice!' they shouted together. It was enough for them just to sniff the aromas of the magical dishes as they wafted by, to feel full. Neither child had ever eaten so well before.

'I feel stuffed!' gasped Siu Yeen , as she lay down to sleep.

'Me too!' puffed Ma Leung. 'I thought you said you couldn't help greedy people...' he mumbled sleepily, as he dozed off. Paintbrush chuckled to see how much pleasure the food had brought to the children.

The next moment, rainbow light filled the stable. Bac Wu had come to check on Ma Leung's progress. He tut-tutted to see the boy fast asleep, but smiled when the Magic Paintbrush

squealed with joy and flew to be reunited with its old master.
The former Emperor gently caressed Paintbrush and recalled the
days when, as a young man, he had first discovered the delights
of painting. The pain of the past reminded him of the present,
and urgently he called out:

'Sleep no more, for danger is here
Sleep no more – your time is near.

The people are hungry, the people are cold
Tyrants grow richer, yet still lust for gold
My bones call for vengeance, my brother is wicked
But all will be well if the right path is picked.

Awake, awake, rise up and make plans
The Goddess of Mercy needs you and your hands
Awake, awake, you children of life
Deliver the adults from trouble and strife.

When gift and child are united at last
Then shall earth shake, and tyrants all pass
Into emptiness.'

The children woke with a start. Siu Yeen screamed when she saw

Bac Wu, but Ma Leung quickly told her that he was a friendly ghost. They paid their respects, and then realised it was almost midnight.

'Bac Wu, how can we escape from Ah Ying?' asked Ma Leung.

'You have the gift, you choose your fate
Magic and power open wide many gates
The heavens are dying, the clouds are like feathers
Your exit is where the snow enters.'

Bac Wu disappeared as if a breeze had carried him away, leaving the children to work out his puzzle. 'Where the snow enters?' They surveyed the stable but saw no exit. Then a snowflake landed on Siu Yeen's nose, and she looked up.

'There, Ma Leung! Look! Up there!' She pointed to a small hole in the thatched roof, just big enough for children to squeeze through.

'It's midnight!' boomed Ah Ying's voice, as she stomped across the courtyard. 'You'd better be ready, or else—'

Ma Leung frantically painted a wobbly rope ladder, as Ah Ying's footsteps grew nearer and nearer. Just as she kicked upon the stable door, Ma Leung finished painting, and the children shinned up the ladder to escape. But Ah Ying gave chase.

The ladder swung dangerously from side to side as the three

scrambled to reach the top, Ah Ying getting closer all the time. As she reached up to grab Ma Leung's foot, a terrible snapping sound filled the air, and one side of the rope ladder came apart. Ah Ying lost her balance and fell backwards, her legs entangled in the rope. The children escaped through the hole and jumped on to a bale of straw on the other side of the stable.

'Sor Ji! Sor Gai! Get me out of this!' screeched Ah Ying.

'Fay Ma, where are you?' cried Siu Yeen. Ma Leung cupped his hands together, placed them to his mouth and whinnied long and loud into the night sky. In an instant, their trusty steed was by their side, and the children jumped on to his back, shouting:

'Fly, fly, be swift and bold
Fly through the air to escape our foe!'

Fay Ma reared up and was off, churning the snow and blasting the children's faces with icy wind.

'After them!' they heard Ah Ying cry. 'Don't let them escape. I want them back, dead or alive!' The children heard the sound of Ah Ying's Mongolian horses breathing hard behind them.

'Faster, Fay Ma, faster!' they urged. Their friend put his head down and shot forward, leaving Ah Ying and her servants behind.

'Get ready!' Ah Ying ordered. 'Aim...Fire!' Three arrows from three deadly bows whistled after the children and the horse.

Ma Leung glanced back and saw the missiles approaching.
Beads of sweat gathered on his forehead as he painted a large fan.
Siu Yeen held her friend tight to stop him from falling off as he
waved it to and fro. The enormous fan made a strong wind, which
met the deadly arrows and sent them back to Ah Ying and her
servants. They turned and fled, hotly pursued by their own arrows.

'I'll get you for this, Ma Leung, if it's the last thing I do. I'll

3 Take revenge bo sow!'[3] screamed Ah Ying.

The children watched their enemies disappear into the night,
and, with a sigh of relief, they headed home.

CHAPTER 12

Ma Leung dropped Siu Yeen off at her house and said: 'I think I'd better go somewhere else. Ah Ying is a dangerous woman and, if I stay here, there's no telling what she might do to you or me. It's me she wants, so, if we're lucky, she'll follow my trail and leave you alone.'

Siu Yeen was silent. Then she said: 'Head north for Beijing. It'll be difficult for her to find you in the capital amongst so many people. Don't worry about me. I have my parents here, and you know how skilled they are in the martial arts. Go on. You'd better go now, while the coast is clear.'

Siu Yeen looked away, and Ma Leung felt tears well up in his eyes. The two friends hugged long and hard, and parted with brave, encouraging smiles. Ma Leung leapt back on to Fay Ma and was gone.

Siu Yeen stood alone, and her tears fell silently and were lost in the freezing snow. She smiled when she heard Ma Leung's voice ring out: 'I'll be back! I'll become a famous painter in Beijing, and Ah Ying will have to leave us alone! Don't forget me! Stay my friend!'

Siu Yeen waved into the distance and whispered: 'Good luck, dear friend.'

CHAPTER 13

Ma Leung's journey took him from night to day, and still he had not reached Beijing. He had to break the ice on a frozen stream before he and Fay Ma could refresh themselves. Ma Leung then painted a Mongolian yurt[1] to sleep in, and, after resting, they continued their trek.   1 Tent Whenever they were hungry, Ma Leung used the Magic Paintbrush to paint food and drink.

They passed many poor peasants along the way. Ma Leung helped them all with Paintbrush's magic. As they approached Beijing, it occurred to the boy that homelessness and poverty seemed to be getting worse, so he helped people more quietly, to prevent another riot.

Ma Leung also started noticing young girls with their feet horribly bound in tight bandages. They hobbled along as if lame, and reminded him of horses with stones in their hooves. He stopped to ask one village girl why her feet were strapped up.

'Don't you know?' She was amazed. 'It's a law – a stupid law – passed by the new Emperor, that all young girls must have their feet bound, on pain of death. Wong Dai[2] thinks that women with small feet look pretty, so we have to be tortured like this,' she raised one horribly disfigured foot, 'or risk execution.'

2 Emperor

Suddenly she stopped talking and stared fearfully at Ma Leung. 'Maybe he's a spy for Wong Dai,' she thought. Terrified, she hobbled away as fast as her stumpy legs would carry her.

Ma Leung felt angry and disgusted with the Emperor. How could a leader inflict such suffering on his people? He worried about Siu Yeen and wondered if she too was in agony with bound feet. He thought about the words of Bac Wu:

'When gift and child are united at last
Then shall earth shake, and tyrants all pass
Into emptiness.'

Was his destiny tied up with the Emperor? This thought troubled him as he continued his way to Beijing.

The boy finally stopped on the outskirts of the capital the next day. He had been pondering about a suitable disguise, so that Ah Ying would not find him, and he had hit upon a most ingenious idea.

'Listen: this is what I'm going to do to hide myself. I'll

continue to paint as before, but this time I won't finish my paintings, so there'll be no magic.' Paintbrush whined with disappointment. 'If there's no magic, then people won't know that I'm Ma Leung, and so Ah Ying will never find out where I am!' Fay Ma whinnied with approval, much to Paintbrush's annoyance.

Ma Leung quickly painted a whole series of incomplete pictures: a bird with no beak, a fish with no fin, and a panda without a tail. Paintbrush teased Ma Leung, making cuckoo noises to imply that the boy was crazy. Fay Ma felt uncertain about the unusual pictures and made no comment. Still, Ma Leung decided to put his idea to the test and headed for Beijing market.

The crowded, noisy streets were an eye-opener for Ma Leung. He felt very small and a little scared. But, with his friends by his side, Ma Leung found the courage to act as if the city was a home to him, and he soon stopped staring so wide-eyed at all the different sights and sounds around him. At the market, Ma Leung observed the stall-holders yelling and touting for customers, and, when he felt confident, the boy joined in.

'Come on, ladies and gentlemen. Buy your lovely paintings here. Fresh from Canton, they're all the rage! A totally new style of painting: "The Canton School of Unfinished Art". Buy now before they all sell out.'

And he was right. They did sell out! Maybe the fact that Ma Leung only charged one yuan per painting had something to do with it, but, rich or poor, all his satisfied customers enjoyed the life-like colours in the paintings as well as the odd quirk of a deliberately omitted piece: they thought it was the trademark of the artist. Ma Leung painted some more incomplete pictures, and again they promptly sold out.

'I'm a success!' Ma Leung thought. 'Even without magic, they like my work. A proper painter – at last!'

He felt sure that, finally, he was on the right path.

CHAPTER 14

Ma Leung felt certain that his dream of being a famous painter was becoming a reality: if they loved his incomplete pictures, how much more would they admire the full paintings! Very pleased with himself, Ma Leung started to paint another picture, this time of a one-eyed heron, and he dreamt of soon returning to Canton and Siu Yeen – so famous that Ah Ying would not dare even to say his name.

The next moment brought disaster. Ah Ying, Sor Ji and Sor Gai ran into the market, hotly pursued by their arrows, which had chased them all the way from Canton. They had abandoned their exhausted horses at the city gates, to try another way of dodging the arrows. The crowds parted as Ah Ying raced by.

'Gow men-ah!'[1] she hollered. 'Help!'   **1 Save me**

Ma Leung stood transfixed. He could not believe that Ah Ying had found him so quickly. But her mind was not on him – every ounce of her body was straining to escape from her deadly arrow.

Ah Ying glanced over her shoulder to check how near the missile was and accidentally bumped into the boy.

Everything seemed to shift into slow motion. Ma Leung was knocked over, and he screamed as he realised what would happen. Uncontrollably, his hand holding the Magic Paintbrush reached out to cushion his fall, and Paintbrush landed square on the last empty socket of the one-eyed heron, creating two eyes.

Instantly, rainbow light filled the market and divine music descended. A ripping sound shivered down the spines of everyone in the crowd, and they gasped as they witnessed a real heron fly up from the paper.

'I'll get you for this, Ma Leung!' spluttered Ah Ying, as she fled from the market, still hunted by her arrow. Sor Ji and Sor Gai had long since skidded and crashed their way out of sight. The crowd gathered around Ma Leung, prostrate on the ground:

'He's the magic boy we've heard so much about.'

'Yes. My uncle in Canton told me he was called Ma Leung.'

'He granted requests to poor people.'

'I'm poor!'

'Me too!'

'Wong Dai has taken all my money!'

'My grandmother and I are about to be thrown out – she'll freeze to death!'

'I can't pay my rent!'

'Please help!'

'Help me!'

'My feet hurt – use your magic!'

'Help me first!'

'No, me!'

'Me, me!'

'Me!'

'Help!'

The sky blackened, and hail as large as walnuts came hissing down. The people ran for cover, leaving Ma Leung alone. Thunder clapped and shook the yellow earth, and, in the midst of this tempest, an Imperial fanfare sounded, loud and strong. A short guard with a big moustache and a high-pitched voice strutted into the square.

'His Almightyness the Great the Good the Wonderful has heard about the magic boy the Lowly the Pitiful the Pathetic and hereby thereto and therefore doth summon this specimen to his Imperialness's home, the Beautiful the Marvellous the Sumptuous Forbidden City—'

'Forbidden City!' whispered the crowd nervously from their shelters.

'And to accompany his Excellency's most Trusted Intelligent and Handsome guard to the aforementioned stated said place straight away forthwith without further ado.'

Ma Leung looked at the guard, swallowed hard and said: 'Excuse me, but I'm busy today.'

'What?!' thundered the little fellow. He produced a ferocious-looking sword from behind his back and waved it frighteningly in the air. Ma Leung stood his ground.

'I'll give you "too busy", you insolent brat!' The guard ordered his men to seize Ma Leung, and the boy was dragged off to meet Wong Dai, the Emperor of all China.

CHAPTER 15

The palace gates were massive. On either side hung splendid banners with the words 'The Emperor lives here!' on the right and 'Long live the Emperor!' on the left. Huge golden knockers in the shape of the Golden Dragon and the Great Phoenix rested regally on the gates. The short guard with the big moustache knocked three times in a slow, solemn way. The knocks echoed in the vast palace.

When nobody answered, the guard rang a tinkly little side bell, and this produced the desired effect. The gates swung open and they were beckoned in. Ma Leung hesitated and peered inside.

All this time, Fay Ma had been silently trailing his friend, and he now realised that this would be the last opportunity to rescue him. The stallion charged forward and reared up menacingly, snorting at the tiny guard. But the little fellow was faster than he looked. In an instant, he had whipped out his sword and waved it fiercely at Fay Ma.

'Back off!' he shouted aggressively. Fay Ma angrily churned the snow with his hooves, as the sharp blade forced him to retreat.

'Fly, fly!' Ma Leung screamed. 'Back to Siu Yeen! Quickly!'

The stallion was torn between staying and going. He reared up and whinnied with frustration. A final attack from the guard forced him to decide, and he turned and fled for Canton.

'You brat!' hissed the guard. 'Why, if I didn't have my orders, I'd chop you into a thousand little pieces right now! But orders are orders – get inside!' He shoved Ma Leung in, and the gates closed behind them with a resounding thud.

As they crossed the magnificent white stone courtyard, a shrill cry of pain touched Ma Leung to the bone.

'Get these bandages off me! I hate small feet! Ba Ba,¹ it **¹ Daddy** hurts! Please!' The voice trailed off in tearful sobs. Ma Leung wondered whom the voice belonged to; he also felt like murdering Wong Dai.

In the royal chamber, silk seemed to be everywhere, as if it grew like a plant. The colours were dazzling: imperial yellow, lucky red, jade green, peacock blue, rampant gold – and more rampant gold. Everywhere the boy looked, more gold burnished his eyes: the throne, the lamps, the candlestick-holders, the ornaments and intricate decorations on the wall. He had stepped into a treasure trove.

Another guard rushed in and, banging a gong, announced: 'Wong Dai is coming! Long live the Emperor!' Everyone fell flat on their faces except Ma Leung, who was confused by their behaviour. Even the fierce little guard was too busy to notice that the boy was still standing.

Ma Leung could not tell if there was an earthquake outside or if his heart, teeth and knees were making the noise, but his ears were filled with a dreadful rumbling as Wong Dai approached.

CHAPTER 16

Ma Leung braced himself to see an ogre, but instead a rotund man rolled into the room, with his nose in the air.

'And why are you standing?' he smiled.

'Because...I have legs,' Ma Leung replied.

'Off with his legs! Insolent boy!' bellowed the Emperor, raising his hand to slap Ma Leung's face.

The little guard lifted his head up: 'Your Majesty, pardon me for disturbing your Worship, but this is the magical boy your Excellency has heard so much about. The one with the Magic Paintbrush; the one the people have been calling "the best painter in China".'

'Really?' said the Emperor. He studied Ma Leung at length, then remarked: 'He looks perfectly ordinary. Hmm...I will test you. If you are so talented, you should be able to tell the difference between these two painters. What do you think of this?'

Wong Dai pulled out some scrolls of Chinese brush-painting from a nearby chest. Ma Leung gasped with delight – never in his young life had he seen such beautiful paintings. He wanted to look for ever, but Wong Dai snatched the pictures away.

'Well?'

Ma Leung was speechless.

'Just as I thought. Rubbish. Well, this effort was painted by the old Emperor, my brother, who did nothing but paint all the time. And now, what do you think of these?'

Wong Dai pulled another set of paintings from a chest and proudly presented them to the boy. Ma Leung took one look at them and wanted to laugh: they were so badly painted. But he had figured out Wong Dai's game, and he carefully said: 'Not too bad.'

'Huh! Hear that? "The best painter in China" thinks my pictures are excellent! And better than my brother's! Hear that?' Ma Leung felt stunned. Had he said that? The guards all mumbled agreement with the Emperor.

'I like you, little boy. If you play your cards right, I might even appoint you "Palace Official Portrait Painter". You'd like that, wouldn't you? Now then, I've heard some incredible stories of you and your Magic Paintbrush. I'd like to see it work for myself – to see if these stories are true. Let me see. I've never had a real dragon before – paint me a dragon!'

Ma Leung stopped and thought, and Wong Dai inched closer

to observe the magic. The boy quickly painted a lizard, which sprang to life and ran up the Emperor's arm to give him a slurpy, wet lick on the cheek.

'Yuck! Get this disgusting thing off me!' Wong Dai screamed. The guards hurriedly shooed it away. 'How dare you, how dare you!' The Emperor lifted Ma Leung off the ground by the scruff of his neck.

'It was an accident,' Ma Leung said innocently.

'Humph! Well, at least you've shown it does work. You'd better be more careful this time, or I'll have your legs chopped off. Now I want you to paint me a phoenix, my own special phoenix.'

Again Ma Leung thought, and this time he painted a black crow instead. The bird immediately attacked the Emperor.

1 Cantonese exclamation of surprise and irritation

'Aie-ya!'¹ shouted Wong Dai, beating the bird off. 'Guards!' They again shooed the creature to a corner of the room. 'That's it! That's your last chance! Take him away!' The guards marched Ma Leung off to the dungeons, but not before the Emperor had seized the Magic Paintbrush for himself.

'You'll never make it work!' cried Ma Leung. 'The Magic Paintbrush can't help greedy people!' He was silenced by a blow to the head from one of the guards and led down a long, gloomy passageway that seemed like a descent into hell.

CHAPTER 17

Ma Leung was locked in a dank, dark cell. A frightened mouse scurried away. The walls were covered in drawings of poems or prayers, left behind by previous prisoners. Ma Leung felt terribly isolated and frightened. He thought of his parents, and of Siu Yeen and Fay Ma far away, and wept.

'Paintbrush will never help him,' Ma Leung thought. 'He's as greedy as Ah Ying. He already rules the Middle Kingdom – what else does he need?'

The boy sat in silence. He was so tired that he soon fell into a deep sleep. After a long while, he was woken by a curious scratching noise at the cell door.

'Ma Leung? Ma Leung, are you there?' whispered a desperate voice.

'Yes. Who is it?' asked the boy.

'Ssh! It's me, Siu Yeen.'

'How did you—'

'Shush! We have no time to lose. Fay Ma brought me to the Palace, and when I couldn't find you anywhere, I guessed you'd be locked up. Who has the key?'

'The little guard. He's short with a big moustache. Do be careful – he has a sharp sword—' but Siu Yeen was already gone.

She searched for the little guard high and low. Her black ninja[1] outfit disguised her perfectly in the shadows. Finally, she found the man lying on a table and crept up to remove his keys.

But the little fellow was only dozing, and woke instantly when he felt a tug at his keys. He whipped out his sword and, with a cry, was bringing it down on Siu Yeen's head when she blew out his candle. The room was plunged into darkness.

Slowly, the two opponents hunted each other: one to kill, the other to steal. Very often, the guard missed cutting Siu Yeen's neck by a hair's breadth, while she was within inches of taking the keys. Eventually, the little man lost his patience and shouted: 'Guards!'

Some men appeared bearing torch lights. 'Seize him!' the guard ordered. The men grabbed Siu Yeen and pulled off her head covering, revealing her face and long hair.

'So you're a girl!' sneered the little guard. 'With unbound feet! How dare you! Don't you know the Emperor's law? Why were you trying to steal my keys?' Siu Yeen was silent. 'Trying to rescue our new prisoner, I bet. Well, you can join him and see how you like our rooms. Take her away!'

CHAPTER 18

Left with the Magic Paintbrush, Wong Dai started drooling over the idea of making an infinite number of wishes come true. Although he already had so many coffers of gold that he did not know what to do with them, the Emperor still wanted more.

'Let me see now. Bars, ingots or coins? Mustn't be greedy! Tee hee! I'll start with gold coins and give myself something to look forward to.'

Wong Dai started painting and, to his delight, the Magic Paintbrush did work. 'The boy was bluffing,' he thought. 'I'll kill him later, after I've shown him all my gold. That'll teach him!'

The gold coins piled higher and higher, forming a large mountain, as Wong Dai worked late into the night and his candle burnt low. He worked obsessively, painting gold coins as if his life depended on it. Sweat poured from his forehead and stung his eyes, but still he painted.

When his candle was almost out, an eerie shadow cast itself on the wall behind Wong Dai. The shadow grew and grew until it loomed directly behind the Emperor. A cry of laughter that hovered between love and hatred revealed the shadow to be Bac Wu.

Wong Dai looked up with a sharp intake of breath. He recognised the voice of his older brother – whom he had murdered with his own hands. For the first time since becoming Emperor, Wong Dai experienced the sort of fear which most of his subjects endured on a daily basis, fear which strikes into the very fibres of the heart and wrenches at the guts.

1 Revenge 'Bo sow!'[1] laughed Bac Wu, and all the gold coins immediately turned into grey rocks and tumbled on to Wong Dai, crushing him.

'Gow men-ah!'[2] cried the Emperor. His guards rushed in and   2 Help dug their over-fed master out of the rubble. 'Out, out, you fools!' he screeched, when they had rescued him from the landslide. He was left alone again.

'It cannot be, it cannot be!' thought Wong Dai. 'I'm the Emperor now!' His words echoed in the empty corridors of the sprawling palace. 'Come out and show yourself, you devil!' he shouted.

A guard with a silly expression popped his head around the door. 'Master, did you call?'

'Out, out, you idiot!' The man hurriedly left again.

'All this magic is making my head spin. I'm imagining things,' laughed Wong Dai. 'Let's try again.'

This time, he painted gold bars the size of bricks. Wong Dai whooped with delight as, one after another, the shiny blocks emerged from Paintbrush, until the whole floor was covered in them. But still he continued to paint.

Bac Wu reappeared, dismayed that his brother had not learnt his lesson from the landslide, and, glancing up at Kuan Yin, the Goddess of Mercy, he whispered: 'Bo sow.' The gold bars linked up behind Wong Dai's back and were magically transformed into an enormous, hissing, golden snake. Wong Dai's smile was wiped off his face when he turned and stared at the monster, eyeball to eyeball.

'Guards! Help!' screamed Wong Dai, as the snake chased him around the room. It caught the rotund Emperor in its golden coils and slowly started squeezing. Just as the snake was unhinging its jaws to swallow Wong Dai whole, a guard thrust a shoe into its mouth, and the rest of the men unwound the snake and carried it away.

'This magic is too dangerous,' thought Wong Dai. 'I shall **3 Daughter** have to get that brat to help me. Ah leoi!'[3]

The beautiful daughter of Wong Dai, Gung Tzee,[4] hobbled **4 Princess** into the room. Her feet were tightly bound with silk bandages, and she was in obvious pain.

5 Daddy   'Ba Ba,[5] my feet really hurt. These bandages are too tight!
Please can I take them off?'

'No,' Wong Dai replied. 'Your mother had small, pretty feet,
and so will you.'

'But I'm not—'

'Silence!' he bellowed. Gung Tzee bowed her head, her feet in
so much pain that it sapped her of the energy to argue.

'I need your help,' said Wong Dai. 'I'm going to offer your
pretty hand in marriage to Ma Leung, in exchange for his
knowledge. You must persuade him to help me use the Magic
Paintbrush properly, and—'

'No.'

'What?'

'I said no, father. You've forced me to have my feet bound,
but you'll never ever make me marry against my will!'

'We'll see about that!' growled Wong Dai. He grabbed his
daughter and painted over her with the Magic Paintbrush, so
that she was turned into a puppet.

'Guards! Bring me the boy!'

Ma Leung was brought before the Emperor.

'What have you done with Siu—'

'Silence! Gag him. Now, perhaps we can talk. I have decided
to let you marry the beautiful Gung Tzee, my only daughter, if

you help me use the Magic Paintbrush properly. What do you say?'

Ma Leung shook his head.

'You'd be the future Emperor of the Middle Kingdom.'

Still Ma Leung shook his head.

'You'd have riches beyond your wildest dreams, the best paintbrushes, the freshest paint, the smoothest paper – you could paint all day and never do a scrap of work.'

Ma Leung shook his head again.

'Look, you little shrimp!' Wong Dai pulled Ma Leung on to his toes by the scruff of the neck. 'Your life is dangling by a thread, and I can cut it any time!'

Ma Leung shrugged. Wong Dai tried another tactic. He quickly painted various musical instruments which played by themselves, then made the puppet of Gung Tzee dance seductively up to the boy. At first, Ma Leung ignored her, but, after a while, the magical music was so overpowering and the puppet so pretty that the boy's senses started swimming, and his resolve weakened.

Seeing this, Wong Dai ungagged the boy and asked: 'Well?'

'All right,' Ma Leung mumbled, 'I will…' Then Bac Wu appeared and conjured up the image of Siu Yeen like an angelic vision. Ma Leung's senses were restored. 'I will never help you!' He kicked the Emperor in the shin.

'Ouch! Ooh! Off with his legs!' screamed Wong Dai. The little guard came forward.

'Your Highness, I believe there is a way we can make the kid do what we want.'

'How?' pouted Wong Dai, rubbing his bruised knee.

'He has a friend – a girlfriend – who tried to rescue him. I caught her and locked her up, to await further orders from your Nobleness.'

'Why didn't you tell me? Fetch her now!'

Ma Leung turned white, dreading to think what Wong Dai would do with Siu Yeen.

CHAPTER 19

Siu Yeen was dragged before the Emperor. 'Big feet!' he cried. 'Yuck!'

The two children looked at each other in despair. Wong Dai grabbed Siu Yeen by the hair and warned Ma Leung: 'If you don't do as I say, your ugly friend here will soon be legless!'

'No, don't, Ma Leung! Remember what Bac Wu—'

'Silence! Gag her.' The guards did so. 'Well?'

Ma Leung thought for a moment, then said: 'Give me my Magic Paintbrush.'

'No funny business, or the girl gets chopped!' warned Wong Dai. Ma Leung nodded. Siu Yeen's eyes bulged with disbelief: Ma Leung the traitor?

'What would you like me to paint?' Ma Leung asked the Emperor. Remembering the previous disasters when he had just painted gold, Wong Dai wanted something which would be foolproof and provide a constant supply of gold. If he had this, Wong Dai thought, he could dispense with Ma Leung's magic for ever – execution would remove all future threat from the boy. Wong Dai hit upon an ingenious idea.

'Paint me a magical money tree that has an endless supply of gold coins for fruit!' Wong Dai ordered.

'Even though you have so much already?' queried Ma Leung.

'Do it!' screamed Wong Dai.

Ma Leung set to work. But he did not paint a tree. Instead, he painted a golden beach and a vast blue sea full of teeming fish.

'That's not a money tree!' exclaimed Wong Dai angrily, pointing at the scene. Ma Leung signalled for him to be patient. The boy then painted a tropical island, in the middle of which grew a tall, glistening tree, heavy with the weight of gold coins.

'A boat, a boat, paint me a boat!' hollered Wong Dai. Ma Leung quickly painted him a grand dragon boat with enormous red sails. The Emperor and his retinue clambered on board, hastily throwing Siu Yeen to one side.

'The wind!' shouted Wong Dai, 'Paint me some wind!' Ma Leung painted the wind, which filled the red sails and blew the dragon boat nearer the island.

'More, more!' screamed Wong Dai impatiently. Ma Leung willingly obliged, and the wind and waves grew bigger and stronger.

'More!' screamed the Emperor. By now, Ma Leung was throwing his whole body into painting, like a mad conductor. The wind blew with the force of a hurricane, the waves crashed up into the heavens, the clouds loomed dark and heavy; lightning ripped the sky apart, thunder exploded and rain lashed down mercilessly. Bac Wu appeared and laughed with joy.

'Enough, enough!' croaked Wong Dai. 'Aargh!' he had seen the ghost of his brother, his older brother whom he had murdered. Bac Wu came right up to Wong Dai's petrified face, smiled, and said: 'Bo sow – at last!'

'Stop, stop!' strained Wong Dai, but either Ma Leung did not hear or he did not want to hear. The boy continued painting until the dragon boat had disappeared behind a gargantuan wave, never to be seen again.

Some say it was blown far away, others think the Emperor was drowned, while some insist that they saw the dragon boat ride the wind and clouds, and sail into the stars. But the people of China were as one in their joyful celebrations of an end to a dark era in their history.

CHAPTER 20

Ma Leung rested in the palace garden. All his anger at Wong Dai had been released. Siu Yeen knelt down beside him and placed her arm around his shoulder. The two friends sat in peace, without needing to speak. Bac Wu flew to join them.

Ma Leung greeted him reverently. 'I've done a terrible thing,' he confessed. 'I've blown the Emperor of China off the face of the earth!'

Bac Wu smiled warmly:

'Oh, child of heaven, do not weep
A tyrant is banished, I am able to sleep
You bring great joy to people on earth
Kuan Yin smiles on her marvellous boy.

Revenge against a treacherous brother

Cannot make me truly happy

But you have fulfilled your destiny

And set the people of China free.

No more heartache, no more cruelty

An end to oppression and tyranny.

When gift and child are united at last

Then shall earth shake, and tyrants all pass

Into emptiness.'

Bac Wu looked up to the Goddess of Mercy, who sent a rainbow
to pierce the clouds and allowed the sun to melt the ice and
snow. Ma Leung's parents came down the rainbow slide and
danced with him and Siu Yeen. Bac Wu picked up the puppet
princess and asked Ma Leung to transform her back into Gung
Tzee, this time with unbound feet. The boy easily did this with
Paintbrush's help.

'Sher-sher,[1] Uncle,' said Gung Tzee gratefully. 'Oh, my poor
feet!' She rubbed them gently, the relief bringing smiles and tears
to her eyes. 'You were right to bo sow,[2] Uncle. My father was a
wicked man.'

'And I trust you won't be like him,' said Bac Wu, unusually in
prose, 'for you are now the new Empress of the Middle Kingdom.'

[1] 'Thank you' in Mandarin (the official Chinese language)

[2] Take reveng

Before she had a chance to answer, Fay Ma broke through the door, neighing to catch everyone's attention. Ah Ying and her silly servants were heading towards the Palace, still pursued by their own arrows. Everyone laughed, and Ma Leung quickly painted a giant dartboard in bright red. As the three exhausted runners collapsed on the palace floor, the arrows plunged into the dartboard.

'Bullseye!' everyone shouted. Ah Ying was now a broken woman, sorry for her past cruelty.

'I hope you've learnt that there's no such thing as a free meal,' remarked Siu Yeen.

'And to beware of loving gold too much!' chipped in Ma Leung. Ah Ying nodded feebly.

'I'm sorry for the trouble I've caused,' she said. 'All this running around has given me time to see how most people really live, and I feel ashamed that I contributed to their suffering. I hope you will find it in your hearts to forgive me, and allow me to make amends.'

'Of course,' said Ma Leung gently. Siu Yeen nodded and smiled.

'I am glad, Ah Ying, that you have decided to change your path,' said Bac Wu. 'And now, Ma Leung, it's time for me to return to Kuan Yin. You have followed a good way, "a path of earth and truth", and the Goddess will be happy to hear my news.'

'Bac Wu,' said Ma Leung, 'don't forget to take the Magic Paintbrush with you.'

'Don't you wish to keep it? After all, it is a gift.'

'Yes!' whistled Paintbrush indignantly. 'Don't you like me any more?'

'Of course I do! You have been a great teacher and an even better friend. But I've been thinking: as long as you're around, people will always want to exploit you, and I may not always be able to stop them. Your magic is too strong and maybe too dangerous for the world at the moment. You belong to another world, a world where things are pure and fantastical. Go home, dear Magic Paintbrush, and paint us a beautiful universe! I'll remember you whenever I see the sunrise, the moon, the stars and the clouds – paint me a golden sunset!'

'If you put it like that...' whistled the Paintbrush, chuffed.

'Stay gold, dear Magic Paintbrush,' added Siu Yeen.

Paintbrush flew from one child to the other, wiping the tears from their faces and painting an even bigger smile on their lips. They kissed and caressed the Magic Paintbrush lovingly for the last time, before it whistled perkily and flew into Bac Wu's hand.

'You have made the right decision, Ma Leung,' smiled Bac Wu. 'But I do want to leave you with some magic.'

'How?' asked the boy.

'With this,' Bac Wu produced his old paintbrush, 'and your

talent. I used it as a child, and my brother resented me for it. Now you may use it, to create beauty and light with your paintings, and inspire others when they feel sad.'

Ma Leung gratefully accepted, and hugged Bac Wu for the first and last time. Paintbrush whistled a tearful farewell, but then, as an afterthought, flew from person to person painting everyone an ordinary paintbrush, with paint that trailed like a long piece of silk, and led them all in a magnificent ribbon dance to lift their spirits.

Bac Wu, the Magic Paintbrush and Ma Leung's parents drifted back to the world of shadows, giving the children one last blessing and reminding Gung Tzee to 'rule wisely'. The money tree started to disappear.

'Ma Leung,' said Gung Tzee, 'I would like you, Siu Yeen and Fay Ma to stay here to keep me company, and paint lots of beautiful pictures to decorate the Palace. You would never need to worry about being poor again, and Siu Yeen, you could even invite your parents to live here!'

Ma Leung, Siu Yeen and Fay Ma looked at each other with the same thought in mind. Ma Leung gave voice to it.

'Gung Tzee, thank you for your kind offer, but we must refuse. You see, we want to travel and share our work...and...er...'

'And my parents enjoy living in Canton,' added Siu Yeen

helpfully, 'but, once again, many thanks for your generous offer.' Fay Ma nodded and blew his lips in agreement.

'So be it!' said Gung Tzee. 'Go out, travel far, and brighten up dull old China! But don't forget to visit now and then.' The three friends willingly agreed.

Ma Leung and Siu Yeen sang an old song about the travelling life of artists as they took their leave, giving everyone a big hug. Then they jumped on to Fay Ma and were gone like the wind, blazing a trail of colour and friendship behind them. Ah Ying and her servants were invited to stay, and they gratefully retired to their rooms to rest.

Gung Tzee was finally left alone in the Palace. For the first time, she felt the yoke of responsibility on her young shoulders. She sat on the enormous golden Imperial throne and squirmed a little. Then she noticed something twinkling amongst the last grains of magic sand. Gung Tzee peered down and picked up a stray, gold coin.

'Hmm,' she said, as she turned it over.

THE END